Two Feet Up, Two Feet Down

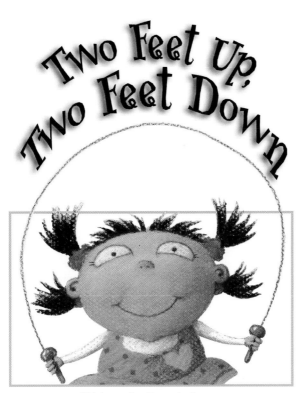

Written by Pamela Love
Illustrated by Lynne Chapman

Children's Press®
A Division of Scholastic Inc.
New York • Toronto • London • Auckland • Sydney
Mexico City • New Delhi • Hong Kong
Danbury, Connecticut

To my grandparents, Russell and Agnes Cushman
and Ray and Meta Gibson.
—P.L.

For Talia and Melissa
—L.C.

Reading Consultants
Linda Cornwell
Literacy Specialist

Katharine A. Kane
Education Consultant
(Retired, San Diego County Office of Education
and San Diego State University)

Library of Congress Cataloging-in-Publication Data
Love, Pamela.
Two feet up, two feet down / written by Pamela Love ; illustrated by Lynne Chapman.
p. cm. — (A Rookie reader)
ISBN 0-516-23612-1 (lib. bdg.) 0-516-24646-1 (pbk.)
[1. In this rhyming story, a girl describes how she jumps rope. 2. Rope skipping—Fiction. 3. Stories in rhyme.] I. Chapman, Lynne, 1960- ill. II. Title. III. Series.
PZ7.L9315 Tw 2004
[E]—dc22 2003018657

1 2 3 4 5 6 7 8 9 10 R 13 12 11 10 09 08 07 06 05 04

Two feet up.

Two feet down.
Swing the jump rope
round and round.

Jump alone.

Jump with friends.
One in the middle,
one at each end.

9

Turn the rope.
Watch it spin.

I jump out.
Who jumps in?

Jump indoors.

Jump outside.

Jump on the playground,
near the slide.

Hop on one foot,
jump on two.

Jumping rope is fun to do!

We jump like frogs
and kangaroos.
Jumping rope is fun to do!

Here's a jump rope.

You jump too!

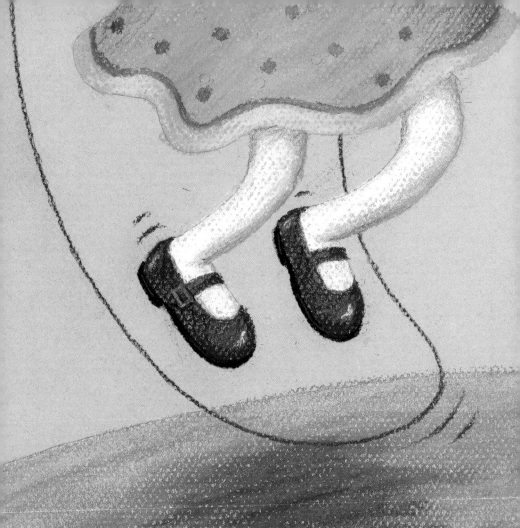

In the air, then on the ground.

30

Two feet up.
Two feet down.

Word List (51 words)

a	fun	like	the
air	ground	middle	then
alone	here's	near	to
and	hop	on	too
at	I	one	turn
do	in	out	two
down	indoors	outside	up
each	is	playground	watch
end	it	rope	we
feet	jump	round	who
foot	jumping	slide	with
friends	jumps	spin	you
frogs	kangaroos	swing	

About the Author

Pamela Love graduated from Bucknell University. Her first picture book, *A Loon Alone*, was published in 2002 with more to follow. Her stories and poems have appeared in such magazines as *Ladybug*, *Pockets*, and *Humpty Dumpty's Magazine*, among others. She lives in Maryland with her husband, Andrew, and their son, Robert. For some reason, she bought a jump rope after finishing this book.

 ## About the Illustrator

Lynne Chapman lives in Sheffield, England. She has been an illustrator for 20 years, but began specializing in children's books six years ago. When she's not at her drawing board, she likes to walk on the moors near her home, play boogie-woogie piano, rummage in used bookstores, and eat hot curries.